Momma's Boots

By Sandra Miller Linhart
Illustrated by Tahna Marie Desmond

The Dixie Lee Connor Award
2005
Daddy's Boots
best children's manuscript

LionHeart Group Publishing ☯ WwW.LionHeartBooks.net
LionHeart Group, LLC
USA ☯ Colorado

Momma's Boots

Text copyright ©2005 by Sandra Miller Linhart
Illustration copyright ©2009 by Tahna Marie Desmond

ISBN 978-0-9845127-1-3 ✦ First Edition April 2010

Printed in the USA ☻ WwW.LionHeartBooks.net

This book is dedicated to my own Army brats:
Diana, Tahna, Paige, Marci & Sophê,
and to all the children whose mothers have gone to help others in desperate times.

Thanks to Professor **Charles Connor** of the Harriette Austin Writers' Group
at UGA for his mentorship, encouragement and insight,
and to the members of the group for their helpful critiques.
"Thank you" to **James A. Bowders**, my friend and military guru
who answered my silly questions with skill and patience.

And, to my favorite editor ~ Teddy Z;
For without his help none of this would have been possible.

~ SML ~

This is dedicated to all the people who've had to overcome trials
and tribulations in their lives… and to my wonderful family of sisters:
Danna Lynn, Peaches Louise, Jo & Jack,
and also my Momma - who've all supported me through mine.
I love you all way past heaven… and back.

~ TMD ~

Momma sits on the couch and laces up her boot. I stand beside her and watch as she pulls the snakelike shoestrings tight.

"Why are you putting on Boots?" I ask. "Are you leaving me again?"

"Yes, Bean, I am." She tucks the laces into the top of her boot and reaches out to me. I back away.

"Why do you always go? Why can't someone else go... just this time?" My eyes sting.

"Oh, Bean. I wish I had an easy answer for you. I would not go if I did not have to. You know that."

Momma holds out her hand to me and I take it.

3

"I have an important job to do in Boots. Lots of grownups do. Not just me," Momma says.

I step onto the toe of her boot.

"Do all Mommies wear boots?" I ask.

"No. Some wear shoes, but their jobs are just as important," Momma says.

"What jobs?" I ask Momma.

"Lawyers, doctors, EMTs and pilots, to name just a few," Momma says.

5

She pulls me onto her lap.

"You know, if I were a lawyer I might wear a grey suit with fancy buttons. I would carry a briefcase. My shoes would be presentable," says Momma.

"My presentable shoes would take me to court where we would stand up for people's rights."

Momma holds me close and wipes away my tears.

8

"If I were a doctor I might wear a white coat with deep pockets. I would carry a stethoscope to hear your heart." Momma puts her hand over my heart. I put my head on her chest.

"I can hear your heart, Momma," I say. "Even without a tetherscope."

Momma smiles.

"My shoes would be comfortable," she says.

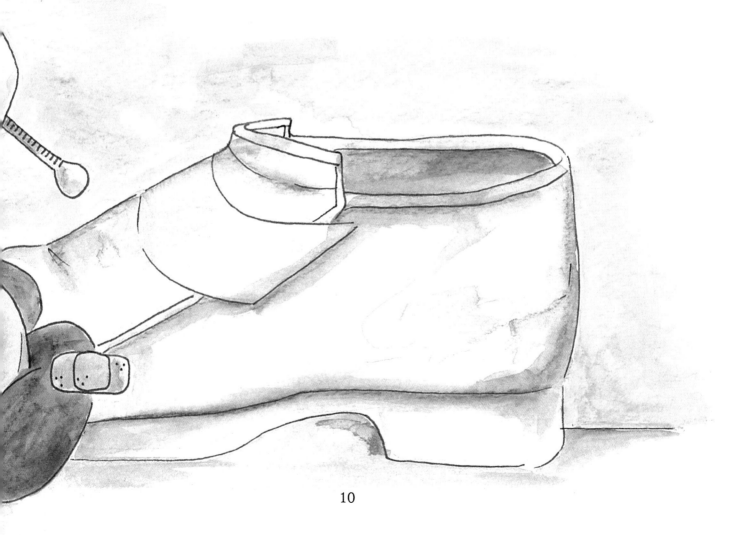

"My comfortable shoes would take me to hospitals where we would stitch people up and try to make them feel better," Momma says.

I sit up straight.

"What about pilots and ementees?" I ask.

"E.M.T.s," says Momma. "It means Emergency Medical Technicians."

"And, if I were an EMT I might wear

a black jacket with bright,

shiny stripes.

FIRST AID KIT

13

"I would carry a first aid kit. My shoes would move fast," Momma says.

"My fast shoes would take me to

accidents where we would rescue

people and try to comfort them."

Momma touches my nose, and winks at me.

"A pilot's shoes move fast, too," I say.

"Yes, they do. They move fast

through the air," Momma says.

16

"If I were a pilot I might wear a tan uniform with wings

on my collar.

17

"I would carry a map," says Momma. "My fast shoes would be ready for take-off..."

"Blast Off!" I say, and Momma laughs.

19

"I would fly a plane or helicopter into rough areas," Momma says.

She holds up my arms like airplane wings.

"...where we would bring in food and water and take people out of harm's way," she adds.

"But, I am a soldier, Bean," Momma says.

"Soldiers wear all kinds of uniforms with all kinds of badges, but we all wear dog tags like these." Momma jingles the chain around her neck.

"I carry my tools in this rucksack," she says.

"My boots are different than any others. They take

me where I am needed and sometimes far away. Soldiers

have many jobs to do," Momma tells me.

"Like lawyers, we stand up for people's rights. Like EMTs, we rescue people. Like doctors and nurses, we heal and comfort them. And, like pilots, we bring food, water and hope to the people who need it the most."

"Will you get hurt?" I ask. My throat feels lumpy.

"I might, Bean." Momma wraps her arms around me and rocks me back and forth. "Boots and I have trained hard to do our job. We have practiced many hours. I know it feels a tad scary, Bean, but I promise we will be careful," she says.

"Can I go with you?" I ask,

and I stick my toes inside

Momma's rucksack.

"You know you can not, but I have your picture in my pocket. No matter how far away Boots take me you will be with me. When I comfort a child I will think of you."

Momma kisses me on my forehead.

"And, when Boots and I soar above the clouds I will look for you. I will count each day until we can come home to you."

"When can you come home to me?" I ask.

I lay my head on her shoulder and feel the bumps on her dog tag with my finger.

"Boots and I will come right home when people have a voice, they no longer hurt, their children are fed and they are out of danger."

Momma picks me up and puts my feet back onto the toes of her boots.

"So, stand up tall. Give me your most comforting hug and your best healing kiss. Give me your love to help keep me out of harm's way, fast and ready to speed safely home to you."

Momma holds me tightly and snuggles me.

"Boots may take me far, far away," she says. "But they will bring me back home to you when our job is done."

Sandra Miller Linhart was born and raised in Lander, Wyoming. She has been a part of the military family community for over 20 years. She has five daughters and two grandsons… so far.

Ms. Linhart's formal education includes Barstow College and University of Georgia. She holds a degree in Sociology with an emphasis on family/child psychology, and a minor in Art.

She currently resides in Colorado, where she is working on the second installment of her chapter book series, **Jones, JEEP, Buck & Blue - Stuck in the Middle**, and the YA series, **Hallie of the Harvey Houses**. Look for them at your favorite online bookstore.

Other picture book titles by Sandra Miller Linhart include the award-winning, **Daddy's Boots**, **What Does a Hero Look Like?**, **But… What If?**, **Grandpa, What If?**, **⇧Mixed Up⇩**, and **Pickysaurus Max**, all illustrated by the wonderful and talented Tahna Marie Desmond.

Tahna Marie Desmond was born in Lander, Wyoming and raised all over the United States. Being an Army Brat herself, Tahna has the unique experience of knowing first-hand the heartaches of deployment.

Ms. Desmond is a formally trained artist, having gleaned visual art instruction from Savannah College of Art & Design in Savannah, Georgia, as well as Pueblo College in Pueblo, Colorado and numerous places in between.

Tahna is currently working on other picture book titles and does graphic art and illustration for commercial purposes.

Made in United States
Orlando, FL
25 February 2025

58913559R00024